# The Grasshopper and the Ant

Retold by Michèle Dufresne · Illustrated by Michael Chesworth

PIONEER VALLEY EDUCATIONAL PRESS, INC.

Grasshopper liked to play in the summer.
Grasshopper liked to sing in the summer.
Grasshopper liked to play and sing all day.

"Come and play!
Come and sing!"
said the grasshopper.

5

"No," said the ant.
"I am working."

"Come and play!
Come and sing!"
said the grasshopper.

"No," said the ant.
"I am working."

"Come and play!
Come and sing!"
said the grasshopper.
"It's fun to play.
It's fun to sing, too!"

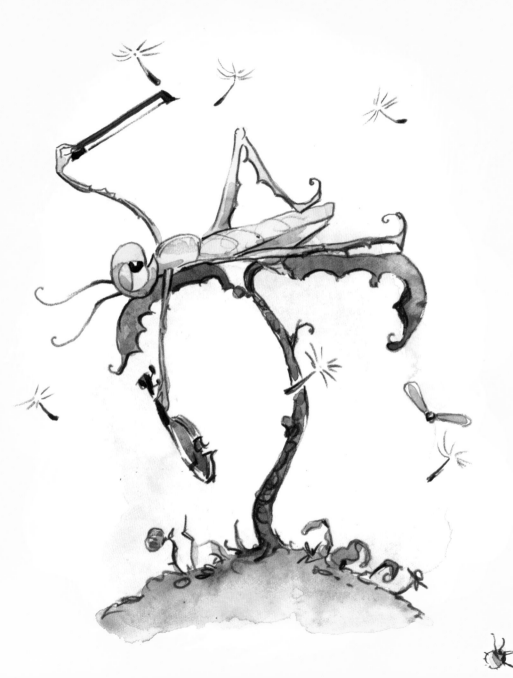

"You will be hungry
in the winter,"
said the ant.

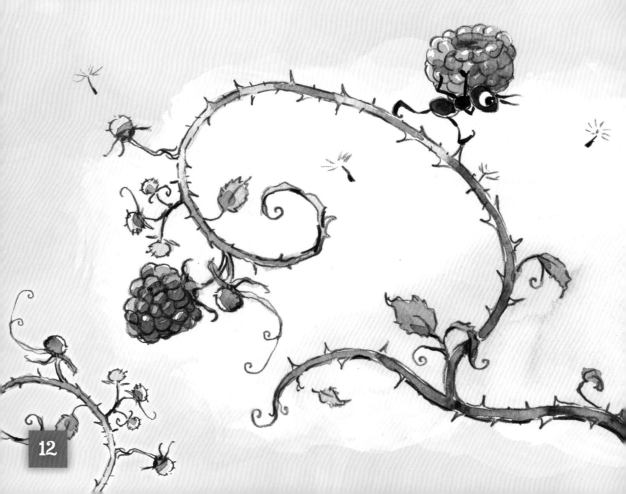

"I will work later,"
said the grasshopper.

Winter is here.

The grasshopper looked
for food.
He looked and looked.
"I am so hungry!"
said the grasshopper.

*Don't put off for tomorrow what you should do today.*